COMMANDER TOAD
AND THE
VOYAGE HOME

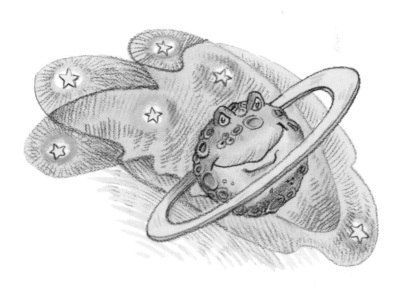

COMMANDER TOAD

AND THE

VOYAGE HOME

by JANE YOLEN

pictures by BRUCE DEGEN

PAPERSTAR

The Putnam & Grosset Group

Text copyright © 1998 by Jane Yolen
Illustrations copyright © 1998 by Bruce Degen
All rights reserved. This book, or parts thereof, may not
be reproduced in any form without permission in writing
from the publisher. A simultaneous publication of G. P. Putnam's Sons
and PaperStar, divisions of The Putnam & Grosset Group,
345 Hudson Street, New York, NY 10014.
G. P. Putnam's Sons, Reg. U. S. Pat. & Tm. Off. PaperStar is
a registered trademark of The Putnam Berkley Group, Inc.
The PaperStar logo is a trademark of
The Putnam Berkley Group, Inc.
Published simultaneously in Canada
Manufactured in China
Text set in Caledonia
Library of Congress Cataloging-in-Publication Data
Yolen, Jane. Commander Toad and the voyage home / by Jane Yolen;
pictures by Bruce Degen. p. cm.
Summary: Commander Toad leads the lean green space machine
"Star Warts" to find new worlds but runs into trouble
when he sets course for home.
[1. Toads—Fiction. 2. Science Fiction.] I. Degen, Bruce, ill.
II. Title. PZ7.Y78Cnu 1997 [Fic]—dc20
96-21739 CIP AC
ISBN 0-399-23122-6 (hardcover)
3 5 7 9 10 8 6 4 2
ISBN 978-0-698-11602-3 (PaperStar)
27 28 29 30

The Hoppy Harris Boys,
Matthew, Robert and Jamie
—JY

For Scott Thomas
—BD

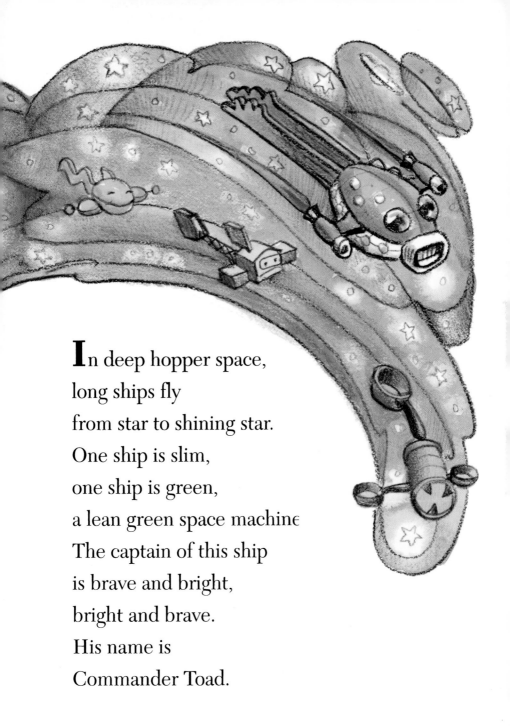

In deep hopper space,
long ships fly
from star to shining star.
One ship is slim,
one ship is green,
a lean green space machine
The captain of this ship
is brave and bright,
bright and brave.
His name is
Commander Toad.

The ship is called *Star Warts*.
Its mission:
to find new worlds,
to explore old galaxies,
to bring a little bit of Earth
out to the alien stars.
Commander Toad is not alone
on his lean green space machine.
Mr. Hop
is the copilot.
Lieutenant Lily
is master of machinery.
Young Jake Skyjumper
keeps an eye on the dials.
And old Doc Peeper,
in his grass-green wig,
keeps everybody healthy and hoppy.

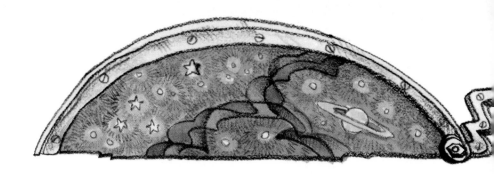

Star Warts has been many long days
in the dark night of space.
It is time for the crew to get
a well-earned rest.
"Let's go home," says Commander Toad,
thinking of a seven-room hole by a lake.
"Home," says Mr. Hop,
thinking about a high-rise pad.
"Home," says Lieutenant Lily,
thinking about a pond by a farm.
"Home," says young Jake Skyjumper,
thinking about his parents' swamp-side trailer.
"Home," says old Doc Peeper,
who has been in hopper space so long,
he knows no other home.

Mr. Hop sets a course for HOME.
And *Star Warts* leaps along the star lanes,
past ringed planets
and constellations,
through worm holes
and black holes
and holes in one,
heading for home,
which is a long, long way
from where they are.

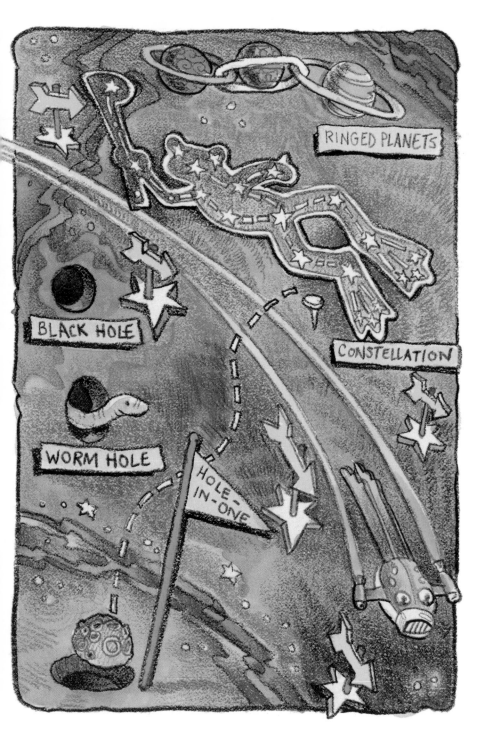

Suddenly the ship stops.

The alarm sounds.

Aaaaa-OOOOO-ga!

Aaaaa-OOOOO-ga!

Lights blink on and off and on.

Red lights.

Green lights.

Christmas-tree lights.

The crew leap to their battle stations.

Commander Toad,
brave and bright,
bright and brave,
looks out the porthole
and leaps to a conclusion.
"This is *not* home," he says,
pointing out the porthole.
There is a planet ahead of them,
covered with strange dark seas.
"That is not our Earth.
Or any other planet we know."
He looks at the star chart.
There is no such a planet marked there.
He bangs out the word HOME
on the ship's navigation panel.
And once again: HOME.
The ship refuses to move.

"I do not like this,"
Commander Toad says.
"The ship does not go forward.
It does not go backward.
It does not move at all.
We may be stranded
on an unmarked planet
for the rest of our lives."
"Since we are already here,"
Mr. Hop says sensibly,
"we should check this planet out.
we are supposed to explore
new worlds, after all."
Lieutenant Lily smiles.
She pats her ray gun.
"I am ready," she says,
"for anything—marked or unmarked."

Young Jake smiles and pats his dials.
"I am ready," he says,
"for anything on or off the dials."
Old Doc Peeper checks his grass-green wig.
It needs straightening out.
"I am ready, too," he says at last.

Only Commander Toad,
bright and brave,
is not ready.
He looks out the porthole again.
"I do not like what I see,"
says Commander Toad.
"And what I see
is a whole lot of sea."

"Whatever happened to bright and brave?"
asks Lieutenant Lily.
"Bright should always come *before* brave,"
says Commander Toad.
"Not in the dictionary,"
Mr. Hop points out.

"I still think we should be bright first.
And that means being smart.
Let's just circle this new planet awhile,"
says Commander Toad.
"My old grandma always warned me
to look before I leap.
And she was the best jumper
in the entire county."

So young Jake sets the dials
for a full planet rotation.
Slowly the *Star Warts*
circles from pole to pole
like a big green pickle
over the dark brine.
"What do you see?" asks Commander Toad.
"Water here," says Lieutenant Lily.
"Water there," says Mr. Hop.
"Water *every*where," says old Doc Peeper.
Commander Toad looks grim.

"Wait a minute!"
shouts young Jake Skyjumper.
"I see a bit of brown in the middle."
"A bit of brown—
and we are down,"
says Commander Toad.
He has stopped looking quite so grim.
He laughs. "I am a poet,
and my feet show it.
They are long fellows!"
He holds up his feet.

Lieutenant Lily and Mr. Hop
wink at each other.
Old Doc Peeper smiles.
But young Jake Skyjumper just looks
puzzled.
"I don't get it," he says.
"Longfellow was a famous Earth poet,"
explains Lieutenant Lily.
Doc Peeper whispers to Mr. Hop,
"Whatever do they teach tads these days?"

Commander Toad resets the dials,
and soon the *Star Warts* hovers
above the brown spot.
"Down we go
to the planet below,"
sings Commander Toad.
The crew groans.
It is another bad poem.

Then Commander Toad and his crew
climb into a small sky skimmer.
They float lightly, brightly, politely,
settling down on the planet's
muddy brown middle.

Then they hop out of the skimmer
and stand shoulder to shoulder
in a toadal circle.
Lieutenant Lily draws her gun.
"Anybody home?" she cries out.
But nothing comes to meet them
or greet them
or fight them.
or bite them
or fright them
Nothing at all.
The brown mud middle lacks any kind of life.
"Awfully quiet, Commander," Lily reports.
"Quiet or not,
I *still* don't like this planet,"
says Commander Toad,
turning quickly to look around.

He trips over a small bump
in the middle of the circle.
But instead of falling flat
on the muddle
in the middle of the brown,
Commander Toad falls
down and down and down and down,
befuddled,
into a big brown hole
in the planet's middle.
"Owowowowowow!" he cries.
"I *knew* I didn't like this place."

Jake Skyjumper leans over the hole.
He can see nothing but darkness.
"Are you hurt, Commander?" he calls.
Commander Toad shouts up and up
and up and up.
"I have stubbed my toes on something."
"Maybe his feet are now short fellows,"
says Mr. Hop.
Jake Skyjumper laughs.
"Now *that*," he says, "is funny!"

"Throw me a rope," Commander Toad cries.
Young Jake throws him a rope.
"Not both ends!" Commander Toad shouts.
But it is too late.
Both ends of the rope land on his head.
"Owowowowow," Commander Toad cries.
There are no other ropes to throw.
"I definitely do not like this planet,"
says Commander Toad,
for now he is stuck in the dark
at the bottom of a hole
in the muddy brown middle
of an unmarked planet.

"Throw me a light," Commander Toad yells.
Jake Skyjumper throws down his flashlight.
"Do it carefully," Commander Toad calls.
But it is too late.
The flashlight lands
on Commander Toad's head.
"Owowowowowow,"
Commander Toad cries,
all poetry knocked out of his brain.

Then he feels around the ground
until he finds the flashlight.
When he turns it on, he shouts:
"WOW!"

The light illuminates
a tall brown statue
down at the bottom of the hole.
"This is peculiar,"
shouts Commander Toad.
"There's a statue here
that looks just like Mr. Hop's grandfather."

He moves the light up
and calls out again.
"On the statue's shoulders
is another statue.
That one looks like
Lieutenant Lily's grandmother."
He moves the light up some more.
"And there's one on top of that,
and it looks just like me!"
"What does it all mean?"
Jake Skyjumper calls down.
"I haven't the froggiest notion!"
Commander Toad yells back.
"Notion, shmotion. You all better
think of a way
to get me out of here."

"This is all very odd," says Mr. Hop,
sitting down on the small brown lump
the commander had tripped over.
He begins to think about the statue,
which means he may be thinking
for a long, long time.
Lieutenant Lily sits on another lump
and scratches her head with her gun.
She, too, begins to think.
Scratch . . . think . . . scratch . . . think . . .
Sitting on a third lump,
old Doc Peeper twists a finger
in his grass-green wig.
Twist . . . think . . . twist . . . think . . .
Young Jake Skyjumper

does not sit down at all.
There are no more small lumps.
So he stands deep in thought
and deeper in mud.
They all think very hard,
but not one of them thinks
of a way to help Commander Toad.

At last Commander Toad,

brave and bright,

bright and brave,

stops waiting for help.

He has been thinking, too.

And what he thinks is this:

My toes are sore from tripping.

My voice is sore from yelling.

It is time to help myself!

He ties the rope

around the statue

in a slip knot

as high up as he can reach.

Then slowly, hand over flipper,
he climbs and climbs and climbs:
onto Grandfather Hop's wooden shoulders,
onto Grandmother Lily's wooden head.
He shimmies up the front
of the wooden statue that looks like him.
But even when he is up
at the top of that statue,
he is still not at the top
of the hole.

Reaching down carefully,
Commander Toad looses the slipknot
and hauls the rope up.
Then he wraps one end
around his ample waist.

He flings the other end
up and out of the hole.
It lands at young Jake's feet.
It tickles Jake's toes.
It brings him out
of his deep muddy thoughts.

"The rope!" Jake shouts.
The others look up,
all their fine thoughts flown.
"Pick . . . up . . . the . . . rope!"
booms Commander Toad's voice.
Young Jake picks up the rope end.
The others get off their brown lumps.
They catch hold of the rest of the rope.
One . . . two . . . three . . .

They haul Commander Toad out of the hole.
He brushes the mud from his uniform.
"Now I know where we are," he says.
They all look puzzled.
"We *are* home," says Commander Toad.
The others look confused.
"This is the original home planet
for all of Earth's toads and frogs," explains
Commander Toad.
"When we punched HOME
on the ship's dials,
Star Warts brought us here."
"How do you know that?" asks Mr. Hop.
Commander Toad points to the hole.
"Because that statue
is a toad-um pole!
Our ancestors carved themselves
in the wood."

Then Commander Toad goes over
to the three brown lumps
the crew has used for seats.
"Do you know what these are?"
"Lumps," says Mr. Hop.
"Brown lumps," says Lieutenant Lily.
"Muddy brown lumps," says old Doc Peeper.
But young Jake Skyjumper
has guessed the answer.
He kneels down and scrapes away the mud.
Underneath each lump is a small statue
of tiny toads and frogs.
"Tadpoles!" young Jake shouts.
"Tadpoles found in holes!
See—I am a poet, too!"
Everybody laughs.

They take photographs
in front of the tadpoles.
Then they take pictures
down in the hole with the toad-um pole.
They take snapshots of themselves
knee-deep in the mud.

And before they go back
to the *Star Warts,*
they leave a statue,
made out of metal,
shaped like a space ship,
next to the toad-um pole.
There is a sign at the bottom of the statue.

Here Our Mothers and fathers Emerged

One small hop for a toad,
One big leap for amphibeans

Having had their voyage home,
the crew sails the skimmer
back up to the ship.
This time when the crew set the dials
for PLANET X,
the *Star Warts* hums and buzzes
and beeps happily.
Then it takes off into deep hopper space,
leapfrogging across the galaxy
from star to star to star.